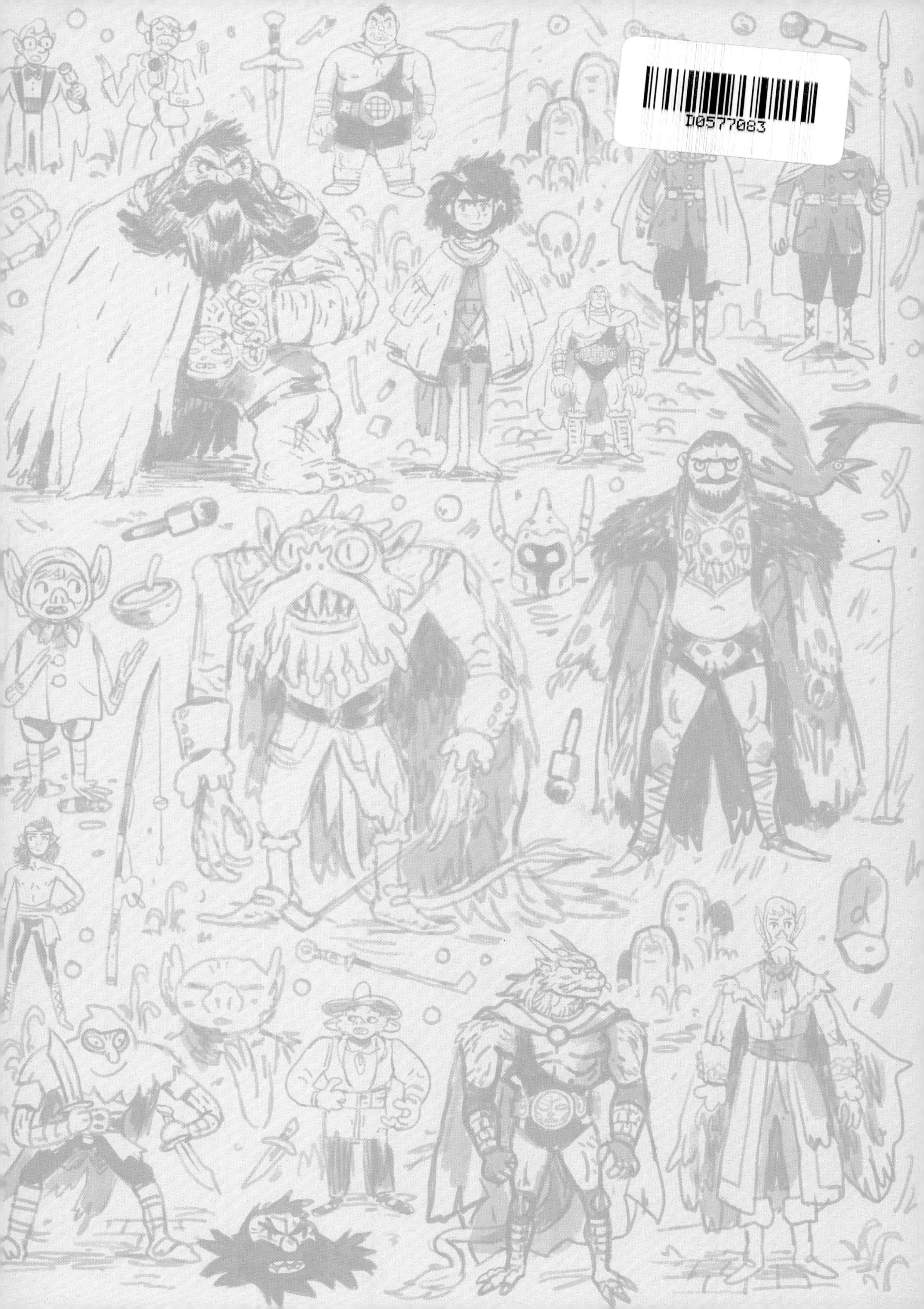

FANTASY SPORTS

SAM BOSMA

NO. 3

THE GREEN KING

NOBROW

LONDON – NEW YORK

SOMEWHERE UP NORTH.

OH! I GOT A HOOK, AND I GOT A LINE, I NEED A FISH TO MAKE IT FINE.

TWANG

JUST A CAN

FISH O' FAVOR, KING OF BRINE, COME TO DINNER, FRIEND O' MINE!

BLOOP

FEH! THINKS THE BLUE FISH O' FAVOR'LL SAVE US, EH?

FISH O' FAVOR? PEH! NO BLASTED FISH LEFT!

NOTHIN' IN THERE BUT OLD JUNK AND LITTLE ABANDONED FISH HOUSES.

3

FISH?

FISH!

FISH?!

FISH!!

IT'S THE BLUE FISH O' FAVOR! I KNOW IT!!

HEAVE!

WUSH

FWUMP

WHAT'S THIS??

THAT'S NO FISH.

NOTHIN' FAVORABLE ABOUT IT, NEITHER.

I DON'T LIKE THIS.

I KNOW A BAD OMEN WHEN I SEE ONE.

WHAT'S THAT THERE? IN ITS PAW.

A CHILD!

ALRIGHT, EVERYONE, MAKE WAY! MAKE WAY FOR THE CAPTAIN OF THE GUARD!

I HEAR TELL A FISH HAS BEEN CAPTURED.

NO FISH, MA'AM.

A SEA-BEAR, BIG LIKE YOU NEVER SEEN.

WEARIN' A BIG GOLD BELT.

BIG GOLD BELT?

IT CAN'T BE...

GOOD PEOPLE! THIS OAF IS NO SEA-BEAR!

IT IS A THIEF!

AND WORSE, AN AGENT FROM THE ORDER OF MAGES!

GUARDS! CLAP THIS ONE IN IRONS.

FIND HIM A NICE CELL IN THE BLACKEST DUNGEON WE HAVE.

MA'AM!

BUT THE CHILD! WHAT OF THE CHILD?!

HM? IF THE WHELP IS IN THE COMPANY OF THIS CREATURE, IT IS LIKELY AN APPRENTICE THIEF.

BUT YES, A CHILD, STILL.

SOMEONE CLEAN HER UP AND SEND HER ON HER WAY.

YIP, YIP.

GROAN...

SHH... YE WILL BE FINE.

MY LITTLE BLUE FISH.

AH, LITTLE FISH IS AWAKE, BLESSED. T'WAS A *NEAR THING*, YIP, A VERY NEAR THING INDEED.

WHO ARE YOU? WHERE AM I?

ME? I'M ONE TO FISH, THAT'S ALL.

AND YE BE IN BED.

I WAS RIDING ON A TURTLE.

AH, YES. THE BLUE FISH IS FRIEND TO ALL THE SEA'S BOUNTY.

SOUP?

GOOD ONION AND OKAY BONE, WITH SOME NICE BARK FOR TEXTURE.

'COURSE, IT'S NOT THE SAME FINE FAIR YE EAT IN THE SEAWEED PALACE, BUT THESE BE HARD TIMES INDEED, YER MAJESTY.

PBBDPTT

WHO DO YOU THINK I AM?!

WHY, YE BE THE BLUE FISH OF FAVOR.

I YOINKED YE FROM THE OCEAN AND SO YE MUST GRANT ME ONE WISH.

YER HERE TO DELIVER US FROM THE EVIL WHAT BEDEVILS OUR HOME, YIP.

UM, I'M NOT A FISH, BUT I'LL HELP IF I CAN.

WHAT KINDA EVIL?

WELL, THERE WAS THE STORM, YIP, THEN THE DROUGHT, THE FAMINE, THE PLAGUE...

THE GAME ALL RUN OFF, AND THE FISH, TOO. OUR LETTERS GO UNANSWERED, OUR COMPASSES DON'T POINT NORTH, AND OUR SOCKS ARE ALWAYS WET.

THEN *THE BEAST* CAME AND ATE OUR POOR KING ARCHIBALD! SCOOPED OUR SWEET BOY RIGHT OUTTA HIS BED AND THAT WAS THAT.

OH! AND THE BEAST LIVES IN THE CASTLE NOW AND IT'S FILLED THE DARN PLACE WITH *MONSTERS!* WE CAN'T EVEN FARM THE FIELDS!

ALL THAT?!

IT'S A LOT, I KNOW, BUT IT SHOULD STILL JUST BE THE ONE WISH, YEAH?

SAVE US?

JEEZ... WHERE TO START? WHAT CAN YOU TELL ME ABOUT THE BEAST?

WE CALL IT *THE GREEN KING.*

A *CURSED BEAST* SENT BY *THE ARCHMAGE* TO WRECK UP THE WHOLE SHOP. A BIG OL' THING WITH A TAIL LIKE A SCORPION'S AND A COAT OF GREEN SCALES HARDER THAN *OLD BAGELS.* IT STALKS THE HALLS OF THE CASTLE HOWLIN' FOR GUTS.

ANYWAY, IT'S VERY BAD.

THE *ARCHMAGE?* AGAIN?!

I CAN'T LET *ANOTHER* TOWN BE DESTROYED. WHICH WAY TO THE CASTLE?

THE ENTRANCE TO THE CASTLE IS BARRED BY A BIG BAD DOOR, LOCKED UP.

NOT EVEN THE STRONGEST *BATTERING RAM* COULD--

WAIT!

A BATTERING RAM...

WHERE'S MUG?

MUG?

THE GUY! BIG RED GUY! HE WAS ON THE TURTLE WITH ME.

HE'S LIKE A THOUSAND POUNDS.

OH! YIP, I FISHED HIM UP SAME AS YE. GOOD FISH DAY.

HE'S IN THE DUNGEON NOW.

WHAT?! WHY?!

I GUESS THAT ONE IS A VERY BAD GUY. THAT'S USUALLY THE TYPE OF GUY GETS PUT IN THE DUNGEON.

WHAT'S GONNA HAPPEN TO HIM?

USUALLY WE'D HAVE A TRIAL WITH A ROBE GUY AND A LITTLE HAMMER AND *EVERYTHING*, BUT, LIKE I SAID, THESE BE HARD TIMES.

SO HE EITHER SITS IN THERE FOREVER OR SOMETHING WILL COME BY AND EAT HIM.

BUT HE'S MY *FRIEND*! AND HE'S NOT A BAD GUY! I MEAN, HE'S NOT *THAT* BAD A GUY!

HE DOESN'T DESERVE TO GET EATEN BY A MONSTER OR ROT IN JAIL FOREVER!

INJURED OR NOT, I'M GONNA SAVE THIS DUMB TOWN AND I'M GONNA SAVE MY DUMB FRIEND.

FIRST I NEED SOME CLOTHES.

I HAVE SOME OF MY SON'S OLD JUNK.

PERFECT. ONE MORE THING.

I NEED A BOOST OVER THE CASTLE WALL.

10

OH, YE LOOK VERY FINE INDEED!

THANKS.

YE SURE YE CAN HANDLE THIS ALL ALONE?

IT'LL BE A CINCH NOW THAT I DON'T HAVE TO WORRY ABOUT MUG GETTING INTO A FIGHT EVERY FIVE MINUTES.

THOUGH HE IS REALLY GOOD AT BREAKING THROUGH DOORS...

GOTCHA

THANKS FOR YOUR HELP!!

HUH!

I THOUGHT THIS PLACE WAS SUPPOSED TO BE FULL OF MONSTERS.

BUT THERE'S NOBODY HOME.

OH! HEY LITTLE PUPPO, WHAT'VE YOU GOT THERE?

OH...

I SEE.

YOU'RE NOT A VERY GOOD BOY, ARE YA?

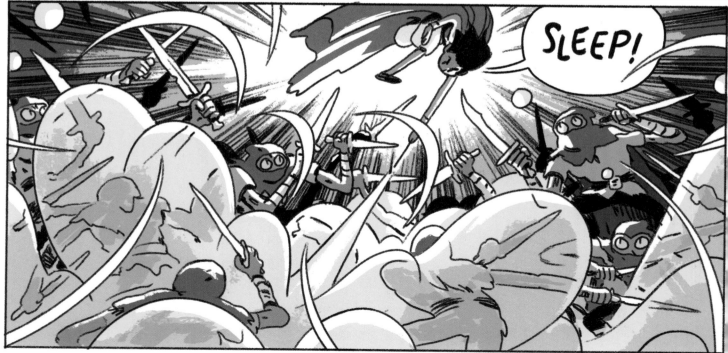

SLEEP!

THINK

IT'S NEVER TOO LATE TO BE A GOOD DOG.

!

HEY! NO GIRLS ALLOWED!!

YEAH!

THIS IS AN OLD BOYS CLUB!!

WE HAVE A DRESS CODE!

THEY AREN'T FOLLOWING ME...?

OH, WOW.

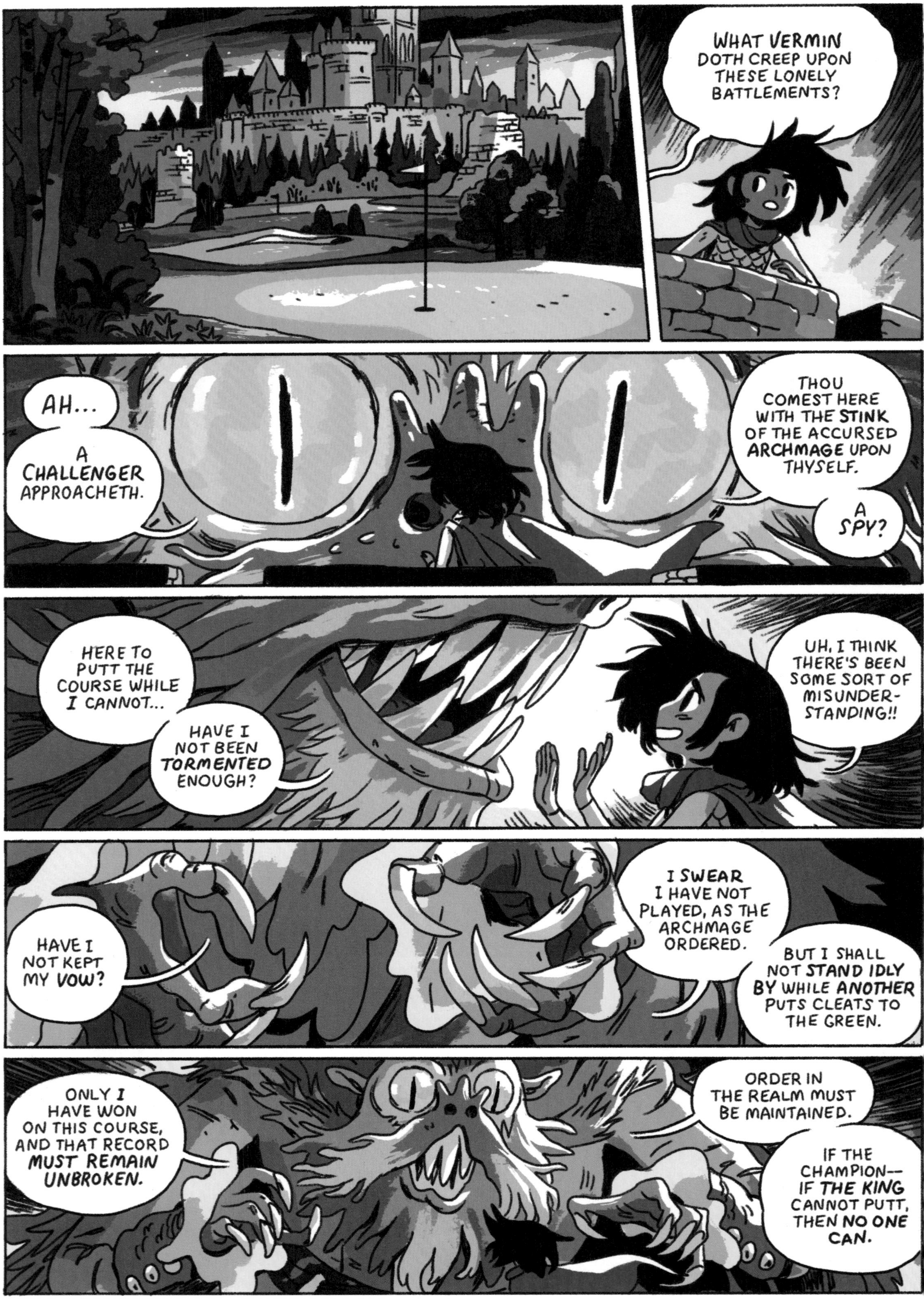
WHAT VERMIN DOTH CREEP UPON THESE LONELY BATTLEMENTS?
AH...
A CHALLENGER APPROACHETH.
THOU COMEST HERE WITH THE STINK OF THE ACCURSED ARCHMAGE UPON THYSELF.
A SPY?
HERE TO PUTT THE COURSE WHILE I CANNOT...
HAVE I NOT BEEN TORMENTED ENOUGH?
UH, I THINK THERE'S BEEN SOME SORT OF MISUNDER-STANDING!!
HAVE I NOT KEPT MY VOW?
I SWEAR I HAVE NOT PLAYED, AS THE ARCHMAGE ORDERED.
BUT I SHALL NOT STAND IDLY BY WHILE ANOTHER PUTS CLEATS TO THE GREEN.
ONLY I HAVE WON ON THIS COURSE, AND THAT RECORD MUST REMAIN UNBROKEN.
ORDER IN THE REALM MUST BE MAINTAINED.
IF THE CHAMPION-- IF THE KING CANNOT PUTT, THEN NO ONE CAN.

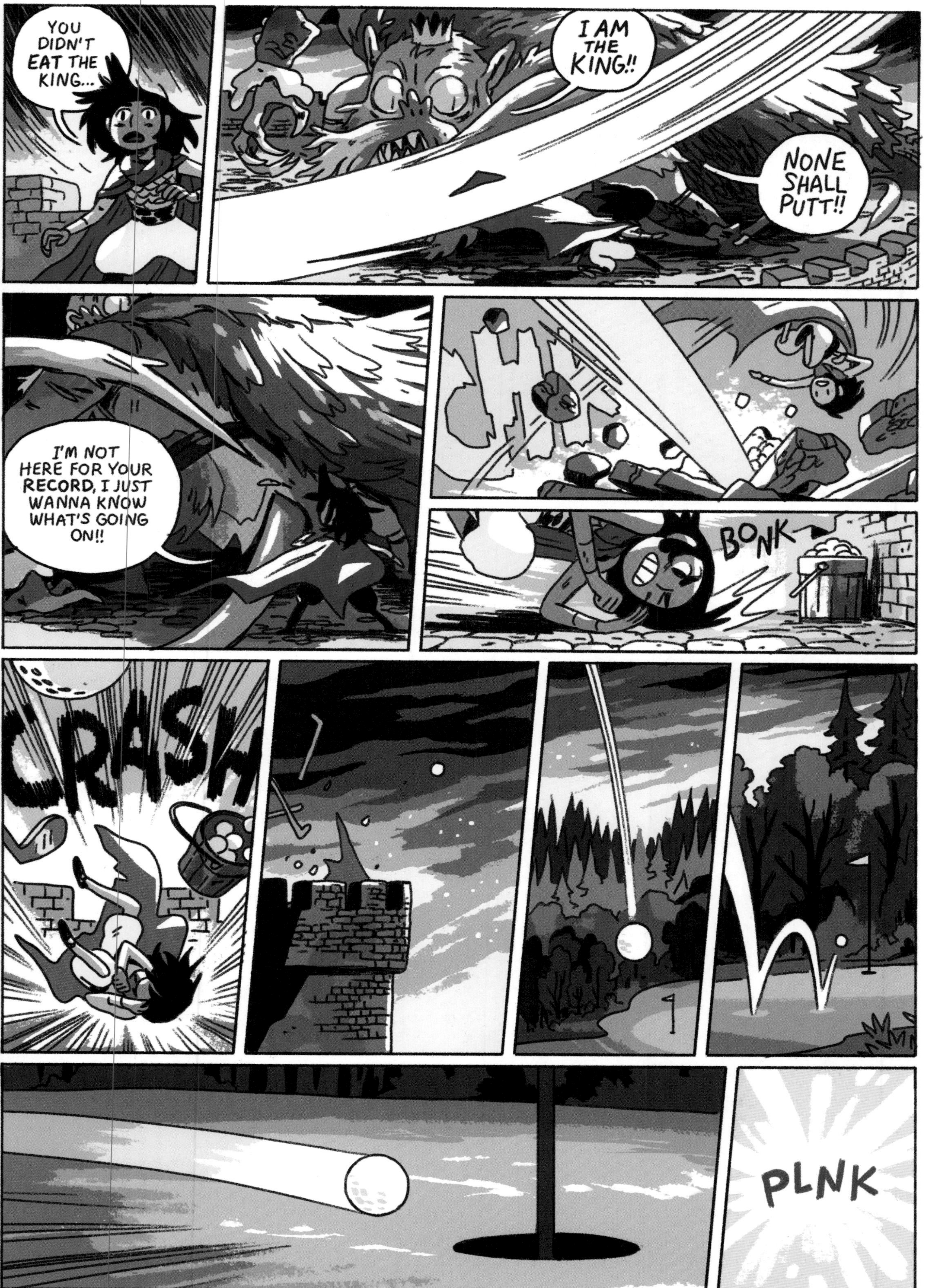

YOU DIDN'T EAT THE KING...
I AM THE KING!!
NONE SHALL PUTT!!
I'M NOT HERE FOR YOUR RECORD, I JUST WANNA KNOW WHAT'S GOING ON!!
BONK
CRASH
PLNK

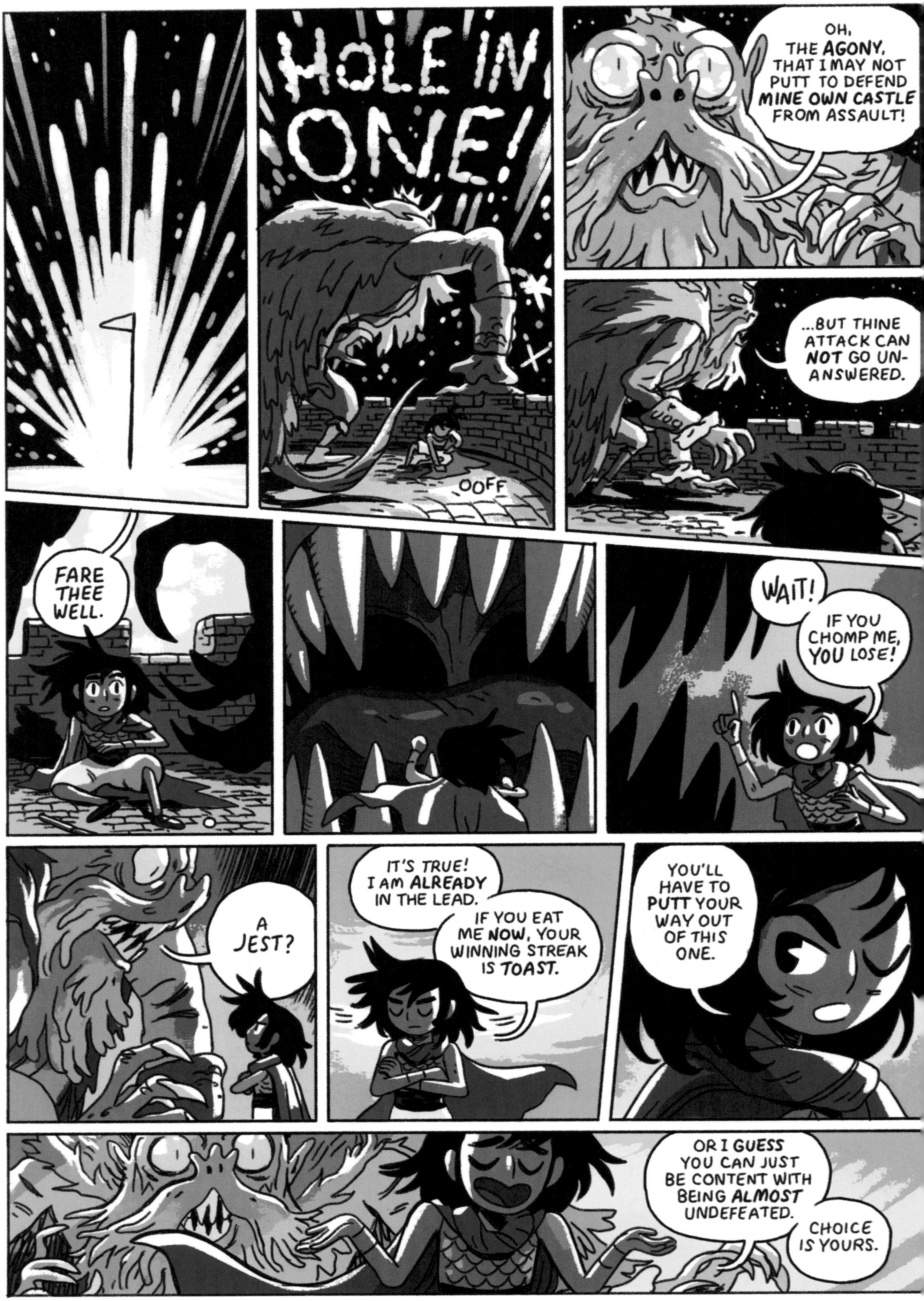
HOLE IN ONE!
OOFF
OH, THE AGONY, THAT I MAY NOT PUTT TO DEFEND MINE OWN CASTLE FROM ASSAULT!
...BUT THINE ATTACK CAN NOT GO UN-ANSWERED.
FARE THEE WELL.
WAIT!
IF YOU CHOMP ME, YOU LOSE!
A JEST?
IT'S TRUE! I AM ALREADY IN THE LEAD.
IF YOU EAT ME NOW, YOUR WINNING STREAK IS TOAST.
YOU'LL HAVE TO PUTT YOUR WAY OUT OF THIS ONE.
OR I GUESS YOU CAN JUST BE CONTENT WITH BEING ALMOST UNDEFEATED.
CHOICE IS YOURS.

MY RECORD... MY **PERFECT** RECORD...

BUT THE CHILD IS **RIGHT.** I CANNOT **LOSE** MY BEAUTIFUL RECORD.

ALAS...

I MUST PUTT!!

CLONK

OH, WHAT HAVE I DONE?

I USED TO BE SO STRONG. A MASTER GOLFER... BUT NO... NO...

I MADE AN OATH.

BENT MY KNEE TO THE ARCHMAGE, SWORE THAT I WOULD NEVER GOLF AGAIN... NEVER **CHALLENGE** HER.

NOW I AM **THIS.**

I'VE LOST MY **FORM** AND I'VE LOST MY **SPORT.** THE RECORD IS ALL I HAVE LEFT.

AND YOU WANT TO TAKE **THAT** FROM ME, TOO?

NO.

THERE ARE EIGHT MORE HOLES.

WHEN I WIN, I WILL EAT YOU, AND NO ONE WILL KNOW I AM AN OATHBREAKER.

NOW...

THIS WAY TO MY GLORIOUS COURSE!

BEHOLD!

THE VILE LOOP. NONE HAVE MASTERED ITS--

CLONK

PLNK

WOW! THAT WAS SO EASY!!

IT GETS HARDER, I PROMISE THEE!!

TINK

THERE IS MUCH YOU DO NOT KNOW.

CREEAK

GOLF IS AN ANCIENT GAME.

IT'S RULES HONED OVER **HUNDREDS** OF YEARS.

THE SAGES SAY THE BEST PUTTING STANCE IS--

YEAH YEAH.

CLINK

I KNOW HOW TO GOLF.

MY CRANKY OLD GRANDAD USED TO PLAY. MOST CRANKY OLD MEN DO.

YOU TRY TO SINK THE BALL INTO THE HOLE.

EACH TIME YOU HIT IT, IT COUNTS AS A STROKE. THAT'S LIKE A POINT.

IF THE BALL GOES OUT OF BOUNDS AND YOU CAN'T RECOVER IT, IT'S AN EXTRA STROKE.

LOWEST SCORE WINS.

HONESTLY?

I DON'T REALLY SEE THE APPEAL.

OF COURSE NOT. THE ORDER *NEVER HAS.*

TOO BUSY SEARCHING FOR *MAGIC* AND *TREASURE* THAT IS ALL UTTERLY *MEANINGLESS.*

HOW COULD'ST THOU UNDERSTAND THE *PEACE* THAT COMES WITH GOLFING?

TO BE *HERE,* IN THE OPEN AIR... NOTHING BUT THE COURSE AND YOUR OPPONENT.

BUT THE ARCHMAGE HATH *TAKEN* THAT PEACE FROM ME.

WHAT?!

SOMEONE TELLS YOU YOU CAN'T *GOLF* SO YOU JUST *ABANDON YOUR PEOPLE?*

WHAT KIND OF *CHAMPION* DOES *THAT?!*

QUIET!!

IF THE ARCHMAGE FINDS OUT I HAVE DIS-OBEYED HER, SHE WILL SEND AN *ARMY* FOR ME.

I CAN NOT FIGHT HER.

SO THE COURSE IS *CLOSED,* AND WE ALL MUST SUFFER *TOGETHER.*

YOU ARE A COWARD.

AND *YOU* ARE LOSING.

20

AT LEAST THE **DEAD** DO NOT SUFFER. THEIR SOULS REST YON.

TAKE CARE YOU DO NOT **WAKE** THEM.

BONK

THUD THUD

PFF

WIZARD...

OOPS! SORRY!!

SORRY- YYYYYYY- YY!!

TINUK

SORRY!!

AHHHH

SORRY.

IS THAT SKELETON GOING TO BE OKAY, YOU THINK?

WHY DOST THOU PRETEND TO CARE FOR MY PEOPLE, SPY?

I'M NOT A SPY.

I JUST WANT MY FRIEND BACK.

Pok
Pok
Pok
Pok

YEAH, I'M FROM THE ORDER, BUT THAT DOESN'T MEAN I WANT TO MESS STUFF UP. I'M HERE TO HELP.

HM?

FUSH

THOU CANNOT FOOL ME, NOR THE COURSE.

A SPY THOU ART.

NOW, MAKE WAY FOR THE KING!!

22

HEY, HOW'D YOU DO THAT??

HEH HEH, THE COURSE KNOWETH IT'S CHAMPION.

HOW?

PLNK

IT HEARETH MINE WORDS AS KING.

BUT YOU DIDN'T SAY ANY SECRET PASSWORD TO IT.

OH? DIDN'T I?

DID SO.

NO, YOU DEFINITELY DID NOT.

DID NOT.

TEST ME NOT, SPY!

I SAID, "MAKE WAY FOR THE KING!!"

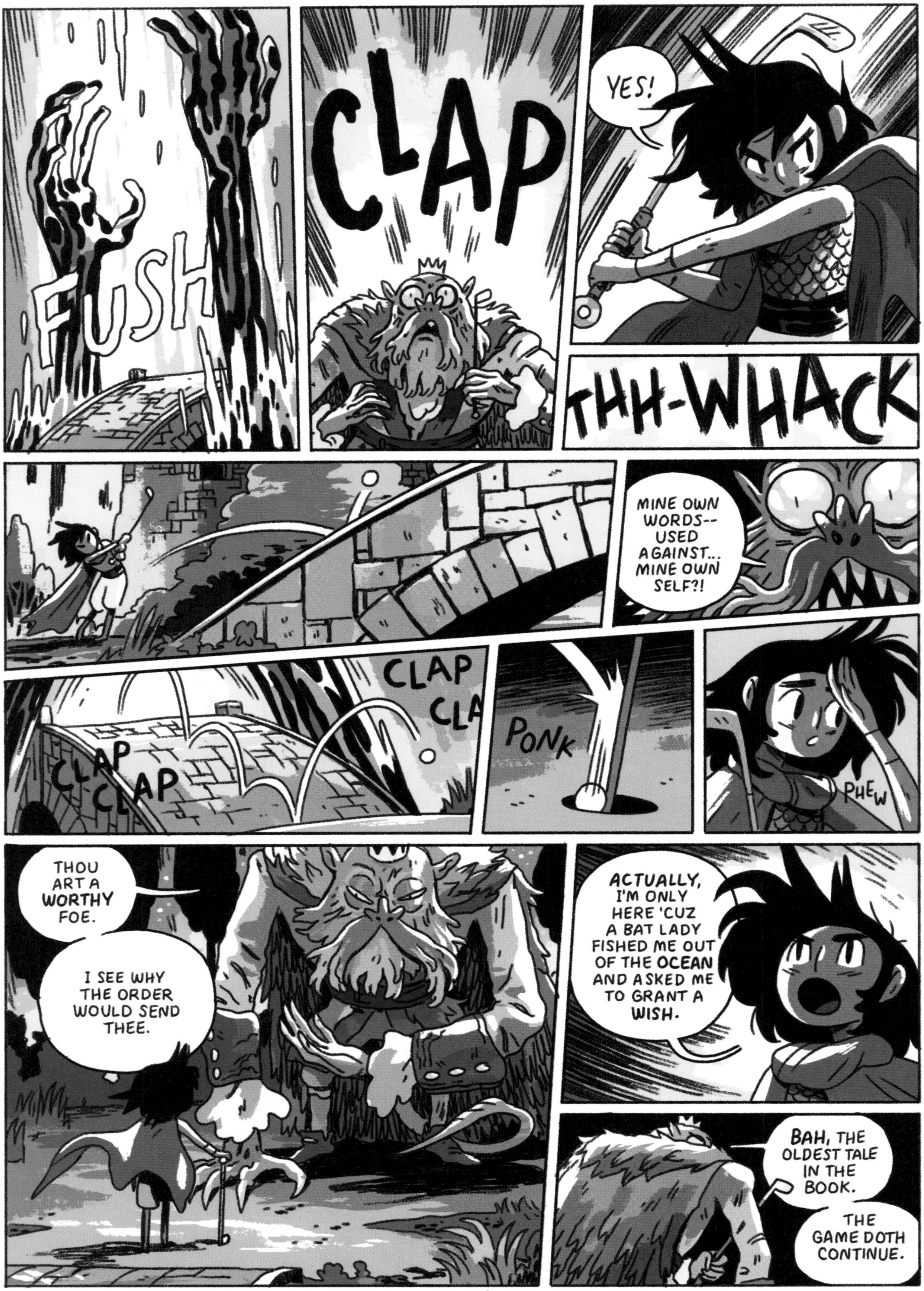
FUSH
CLAP
YES!
THH-WHACK
MINE OWN WORDS-- USED AGAINST... MINE OWN SELF?!
CLAP CLAP
CLAP CLA
PONK
PHEW
THOU ART A WORTHY FOE.
I SEE WHY THE ORDER WOULD SEND THEE.
ACTUALLY, I'M ONLY HERE 'CUZ A BAT LADY FISHED ME OUT OF THE OCEAN AND ASKED ME TO GRANT A WISH.
BAH, THE OLDEST TALE IN THE BOOK.
THE GAME DOTH CONTINUE.

JEEZ!

YOU SURE HAVE A LOT OF SPOOKY TOWERS, HUH?

WITH ALL THESE STAIRS, YOU MUST HAVE A SUPER STRONG BUTT!

THOU SPEAK'ST SO TO A KING?!

KINGS CAN'T HAVE STRONG BUTTS?

THAT MISSETH THE POINT.

WHOA, THERE'S ALL SORTS OF COOL OLD STUFF IN HERE!

KINDA WEIRD TO HAVE A HOLE IN HERE...

CLONK

OH, DANG.

I'LL NEVER BE ABLE TO HIT IT THAT FAR.

HMMM-MMMMM-MMMM.

HEY, UM, IS IT OKAY IF I MOVE SOME STUFF?

SUCH A WEAK CHILD COULD'ST DO NO HARM HERE.

SCREEAK

-SHOVE-

OKIE DOKIE.

BOOM

UH, SORRY ABOUT YOUR WALL.

WHAT RECKLESS DESTRUCTION THOU HAST WROUGHT.

YEAH...

MUG WOULD'VE LOVED IT...

♫OHHH

WHEN THE WAR IS OVER, LOVE, AND PEACE ON EVERY SHORE...

WE COME BACK TO OUR FAMILIES AND THE GAMES THAT WE ADORE...

WE FILL OUR CUPS AND EAT OUR FILL AND SPEND OUR MONEY FREE...

AND WHEN THE MONEY'S ALL RUN OUT, WE'LL GO RIGHT BACK TO SEA.

YOU HAVE A LOVELY VOICE. PITY NO ONE ELSE CAN HEAR IT.

FINALLY COME TO PUT ME OUTTA MY MISERY, ARE YA?

HA! NOT EVERY- ONE IS A CROOK LIKE YOU.

I'M HERE FOR THE BELT.

THE STOLEN BELT.

WHAT'S STOLEN? THIS?

IT'S MINE.

THAT BELONGED TO A FRIEND OF MINE. A GOOD MAN.

BY THE WOMAN WHO CALLS HERSELF ARCHMAGE.

IT WAS STOLEN A LONG TIME AGO...

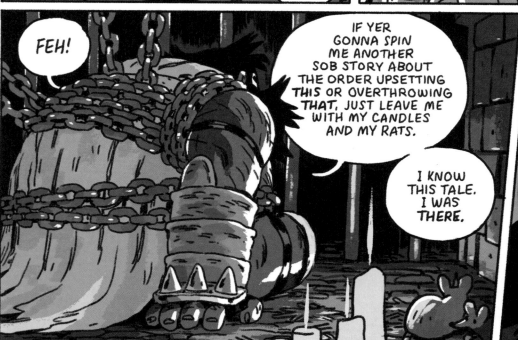

FEH!

IF YER GONNA SPIN ME ANOTHER SOB STORY ABOUT THE ORDER UPSETTING THIS OR OVERTHROWING THAT, JUST LEAVE ME WITH MY CANDLES AND MY RATS.

I KNOW THIS TALE. I WAS THERE.

I SAW OUR CHAMPION TURN HIS HEEL. SAW HIM GO BAD.

GOLDENROD.

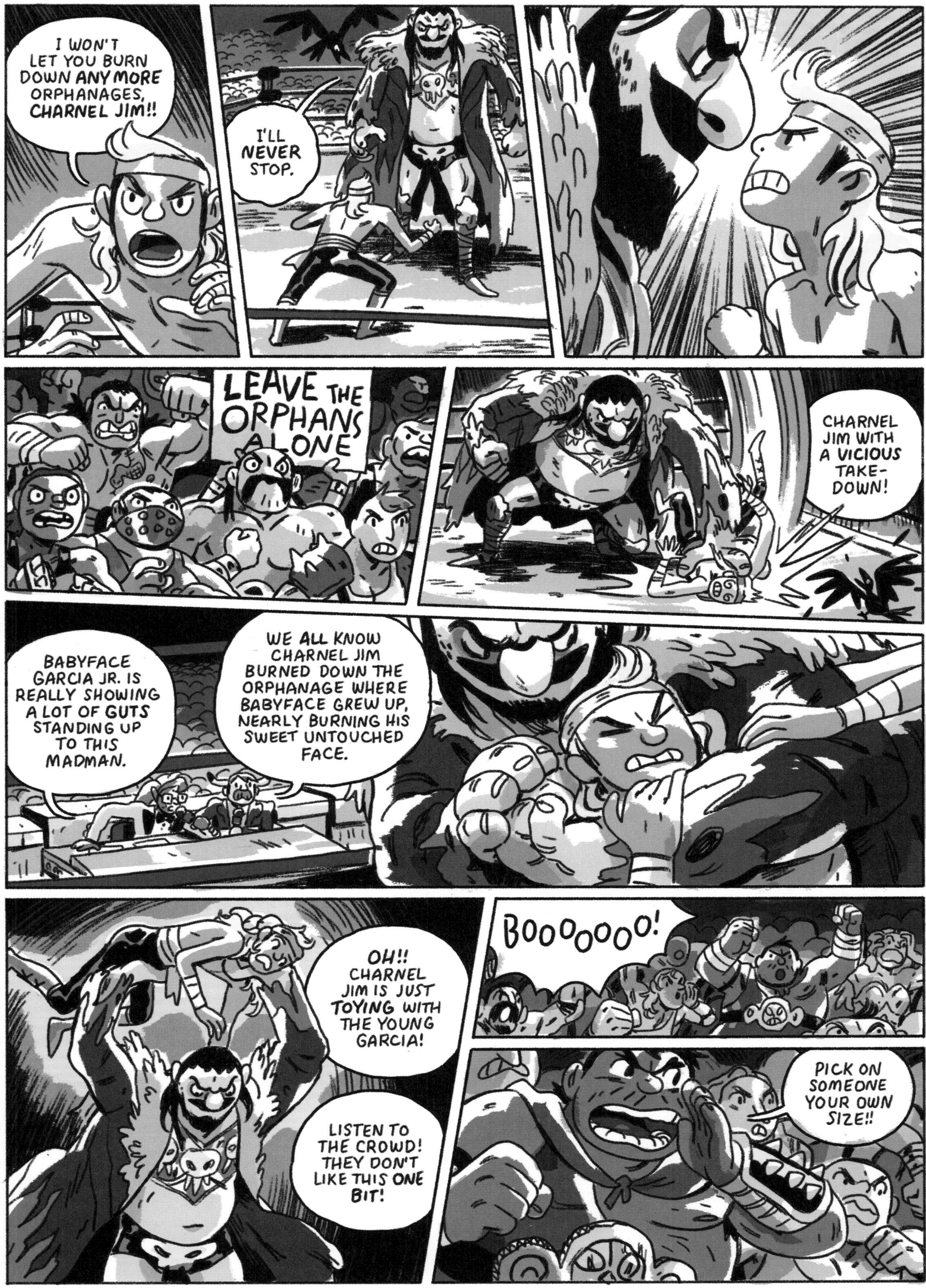
I WON'T LET YOU BURN DOWN ANY MORE ORPHANAGES, CHARNEL JIM!!
I'LL NEVER STOP.
LEAVE THE ORPHANS ALONE
CHARNEL JIM WITH A VICIOUS TAKE-DOWN!
BABYFACE GARCIA JR. IS REALLY SHOWING A LOT OF GUTS STANDING UP TO THIS MADMAN.
WE ALL KNOW CHARNEL JIM BURNED DOWN THE ORPHANAGE WHERE BABYFACE GREW UP, NEARLY BURNING HIS SWEET UNTOUCHED FACE.
OH!! CHARNEL JIM IS JUST TOYING WITH THE YOUNG GARCIA!
LISTEN TO THE CROWD! THEY DON'T LIKE THIS ONE BIT!
BOOOOOOO!
PICK ON SOMEONE YOUR OWN SIZE!!

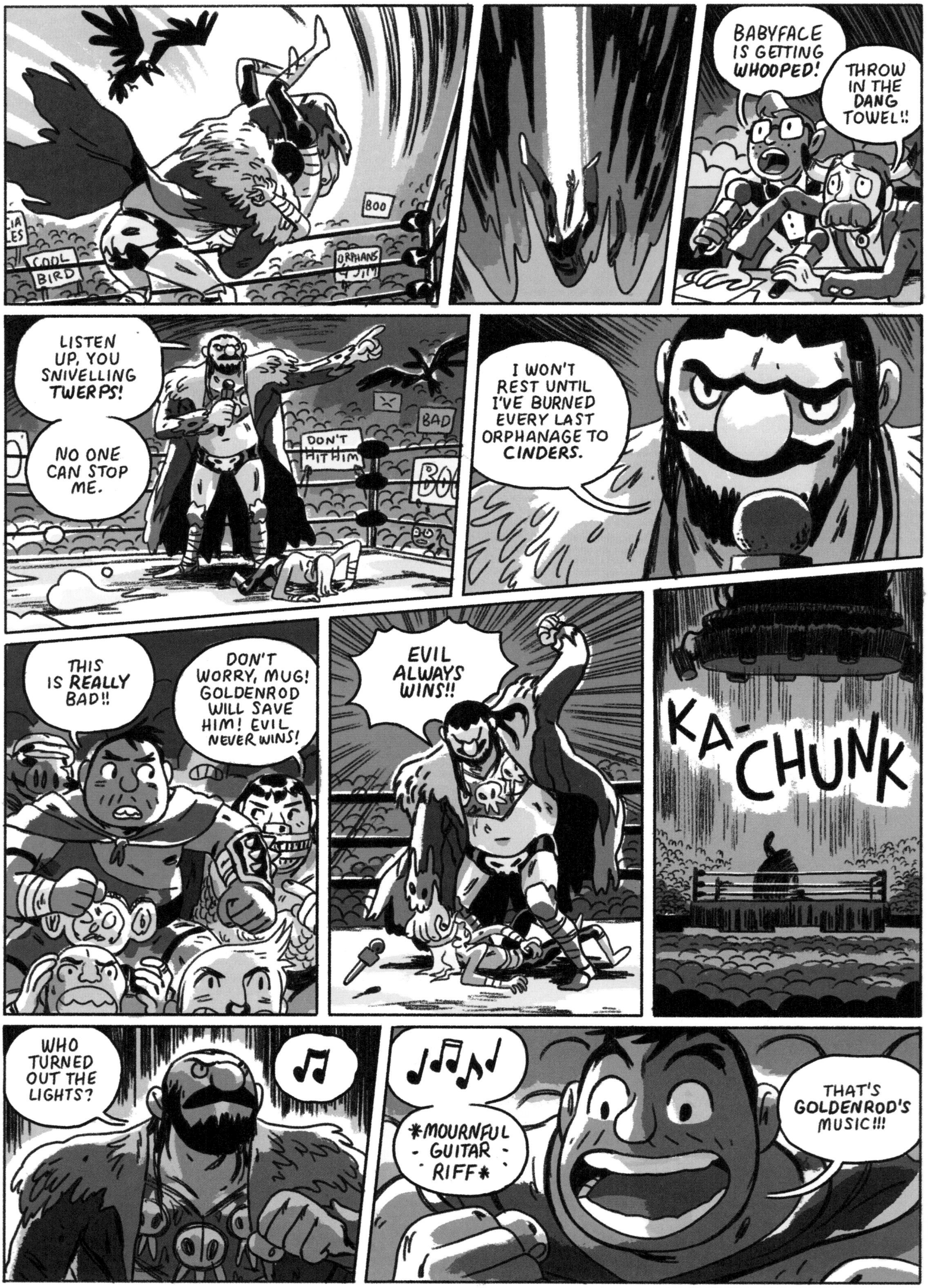
CIA
LES
COOL BIRD
BOO
ORPHANS 4 JIM
BABYFACE IS GETTING WHOOPED!
THROW IN THE DANG TOWEL!!
LISTEN UP, YOU SNIVELLING TWERPS!
NO ONE CAN STOP ME.
DON'T HIT HIM
BAD
BOO
I WON'T REST UNTIL I'VE BURNED EVERY LAST ORPHANAGE TO CINDERS.
THIS IS REALLY BAD!!
DON'T WORRY, MUG! GOLDENROD WILL SAVE HIM! EVIL NEVER WINS!
EVIL ALWAYS WINS!!
KA-CHUNK
WHO TURNED OUT THE LIGHTS?
MOURNFUL GUITAR RIFF
THAT'S GOLDENROD'S MUSIC!!!

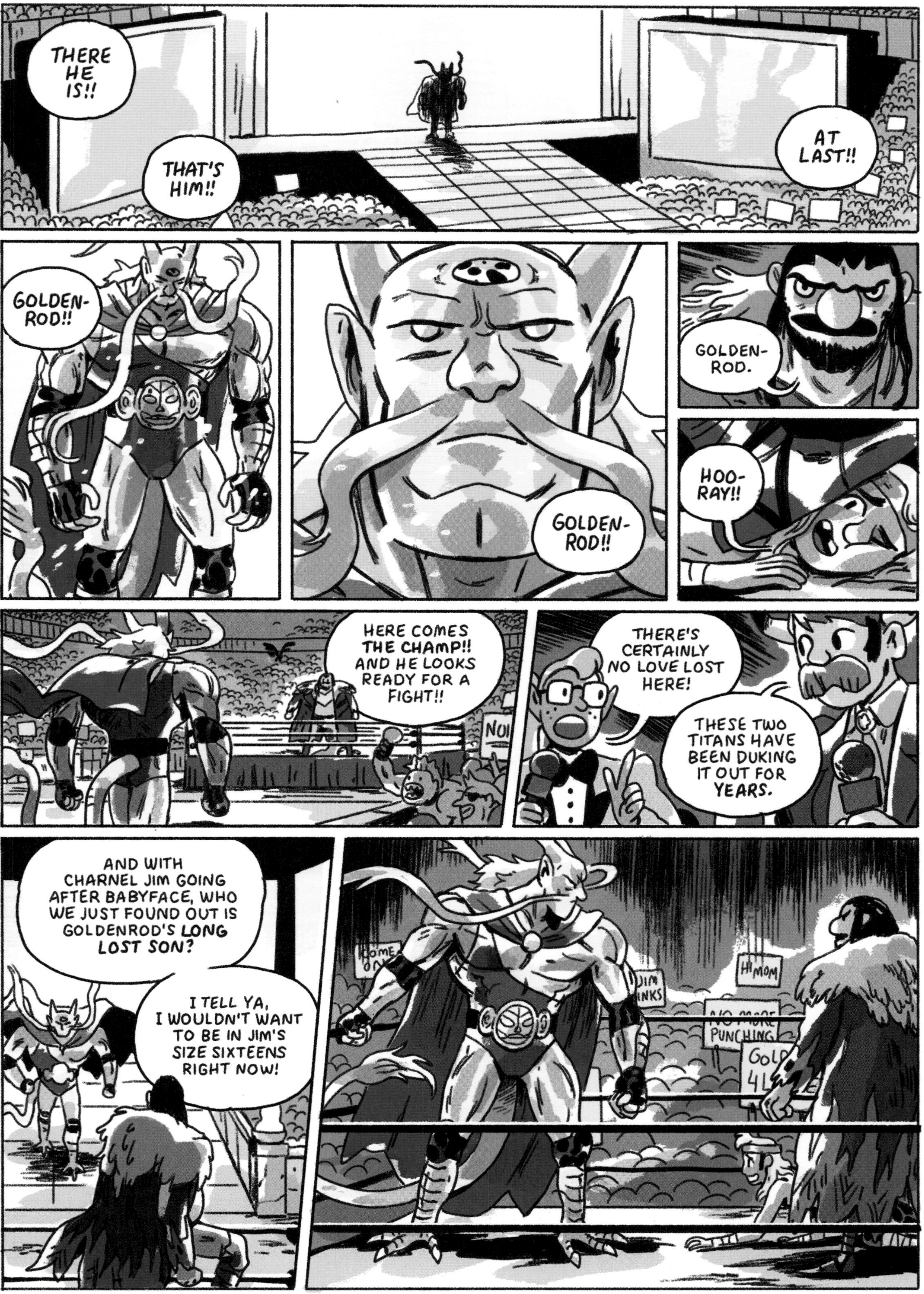
THERE HE IS!!
THAT'S HIM!!
AT LAST!!
GOLDEN-ROD!!
GOLDEN-ROD!!
GOLDEN-ROD.
HOO-RAY!!
HERE COMES THE CHAMP!! AND HE LOOKS READY FOR A FIGHT!!
THERE'S CERTAINLY NO LOVE LOST HERE!
THESE TWO TITANS HAVE BEEN DUKING IT OUT FOR YEARS.
AND WITH CHARNEL JIM GOING AFTER BABYFACE, WHO WE JUST FOUND OUT IS GOLDENROD'S LONG LOST SON?
I TELL YA, I WOULDN'T WANT TO BE IN JIM'S SIZE SIXTEENS RIGHT NOW!
HI MOM
NO MORE PUNCHING

CHARNEL JIM, MY ARCH NEMESIS. THE BADDEST MAN ON THE BLOCK. HOW LONG ARE WE GONNA KEEP DOING THIS?

YOU STOLE THE QUEEN'S WHEELCHAIR. YOU BRAINWASHED RICKY LIONHEART INTO JOINING YOUR CULT. HELL, YOU FROZE YOUR OWN FATHER IN A BLOCK OF ICE.

EVERY TIME, I BEAT YOU.

AND EVERY TIME, I COME BACK STRONGER.

EXACTLY! AND YOU KNOW WHAT I'VE LEARNED?

NOTHING STAYS SAVED.

PHEW

YOU CAN'T BEAT THE DEVIL!!

WHAT?!

GOLDENROD!!

POPPA... WHY?!

I'M *SICK* OF PROTECTING THE WEAK.

THIS CAN'T BE HAPPENING!

CHARNEL JIM IS *RIGHT.* EVIL ALWAYS WINS.

AND I AM A WINNER.

WHAT'S GOING ON?!

CHARNEL JIM UP ON THE TURNBUCKLE. WHAT IN THE WORLD IS HE--

FOR THE LOVE OF GOD, NO!!

THE LEG DROP! LEG DROP FROM THE *TOP* ROPE!!

BOO

SHOW YOUR CHAMPION SOME RESPECT, YOU LOUSY YOKELS.

IT'S TIME FOR A NEW WORLD ORDER, AND IT STARTS HERE, WITH MY WEAKLING SON.

BUT HE WAS ONLY THE BEGINNING.

YOU'RE NEXT.

YOU'RE ALL NEXT!!

LADIES AND GENTS, THIS IS A DARK DAY.

OUR CHAMPION, OUR GUIDING LIGHT...

HAS TURNED EVIL.

NOW WE MUST PREPARE FOR AN ERA OF SHADOW AND BLOOD, THE LIKES OF WHICH WE'VE NEVER SEEN.

WOULDN'T YOU SAY SO, CHUCK?

IF WE'RE LUCK--

KA-BOOM

AND THERE SHE WAS.

THE ARCHMAGE.

FWOOM

AND THAT WAS THE END.

THE ORDER WIPED BOTH OF THOSE GUYS OFF THE MAP. MY HERO TURNED INTO A MONSTER, BUT THE GOOD GUYS WON.

I PLEDGED MY *LIFE* TO THE ORDER *RIGHT* THERE.

I GUESS WE SHOULD'A SEEN IT COMING EARLIER.

GOLDENROD WAS WINNING MATCHES LEFT AND RIGHT, RACKING UP TITLES.

TAG TEAM, HEAVYWEIGHT, ULTRA-HEAVYWEIGHT, ULTRA-MEGA HEAVY-WEIGHT, AND WITH EACH ONE, A BIG GOLD BELT.

ONLY A MATTER A' TIME BEFORE THEY DROVE 'IM MAD.

IT HAPPENS TO A LOT OF CHAMPIONS. GLORY GOES TO THEIR HEADS.

THAT'S WHY THE ORDER EXISTS.

YOU *REALLY* DIDN'T KNOW...

KNOW *WHAT?!*

IT WASN'T REAL.

GOLDEN-ROD, CHARNEL JIM, THE FEUDS, THE *FIGHTS*... IT WAS ALL A STORY.

YA MEAN FAKED?

SEZ WHO?

WE HAD A GREAT SCRIPT.

GOLDENROD WOULD TURN EVIL, THEN, AFTER A LITTLE WHILE, HE WOULD COME TO HIS SENSES.

ONE MORE VICTIM OF CHARNEL JIM'S MIND-CONTROL SPELL.

NAH, MIND CONTROL NEVER WORKED ON GOLDENROD BEFORE.

BUT FINDING OUT ABOUT HIS LONG-LOST SON SOFTENED GOLDENROD'S HEART.

IT GAVE JIM A WAY IN.

GOLDENROD ALWAYS DID HAVE A SOFT SPOT FOR--

HEY! YER NOT GONNA TRICK ME THAT EASY.

HERE. TAKE A LOOK AT THIS.

AN OLD FAMILY PHOTO.

EH?

THAT'S ME AND MY FATHER—CHARNEL JIM...

AND MY FATHER'S BEST FRIEND. I THINK YOU KNOW HIM.

YOU LOST YOUR HERO, AND I LOST MY FAMILY.

THE ARCHMAGE KNEW IT WAS A PERFORMANCE AND DESTROYED THEM ANY WAY.

YOU'VE BEEN LIED TO.

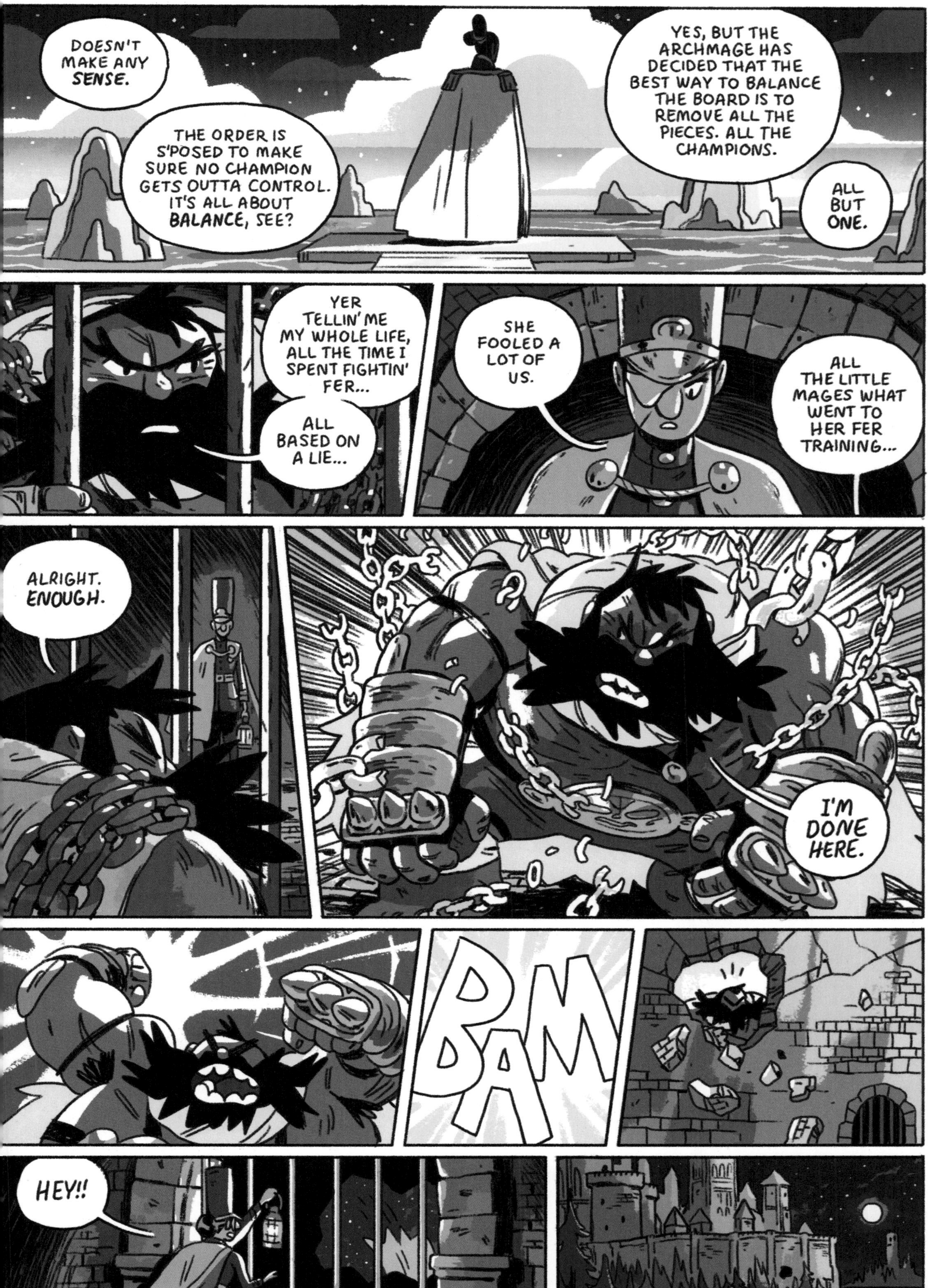
DOESN'T MAKE ANY SENSE.
THE ORDER IS S'POSED TO MAKE SURE NO CHAMPION GETS OUTTA CONTROL. IT'S ALL ABOUT BALANCE, SEE?
YES, BUT THE ARCHMAGE HAS DECIDED THAT THE BEST WAY TO BALANCE THE BOARD IS TO REMOVE ALL THE PIECES. ALL THE CHAMPIONS.
ALL BUT ONE.
YER TELLIN' ME MY WHOLE LIFE, ALL THE TIME I SPENT FIGHTIN' FER...
ALL BASED ON A LIE...
SHE FOOLED A LOT OF US.
ALL THE LITTLE MAGES WHAT WENT TO HER FER TRAINING...
ALRIGHT. ENOUGH.
I'M DONE HERE.
BAM
HEY!!

SHOO! BEAT IT! SCRAM!!

I'M GOLFIN' HERE!!

ACK-- BUGS, TOO??
OH!

PLNK

THY SKILL HAS BEEN IMPRESSIVE INDEED.

PERHAPS THOU SEEK'ST TO BECOME A **CHAMPION** THYSELF?

I'VE THOUGHT ABOUT IT, BUT IT SCARES ME.

MAYBE THE PRESSURE WOULD BE TOO MUCH.

WHAT IF I CAN'T HANDLE IT?

WHAT IF I'M BAD ON THE **INSIDE** AND THE POWER JUST BRINGS IT OUT?

WHAT IF I FORGET?

FORGET **WHAT?** FORGET HOW TO WIN?

FORGET ABOUT THE PEOPLE I'M PLAYING FOR.

SO I DON'T--

HUH?

WHO'S THIS GUY?

THE BLACK IRON HEADS-MAN.

GUARDIAN OF THE EIGHTH HOLE.

OH.

~sigh YEAH, OKAY.

I GUESS THE HOLE IS PAST HIM?

YES... BEYOND HIM, THROUGH A TUNNEL IN THE GREAT TREE.

IF THOU ART JUDGED **WORTHY**, HE WILL STEP ASIDE.

WHO'S HE TO JUDGE? HE DOESN'T KNOW ME.

HMPH.

CREEE**EAK**!

THOU ART JUDGED...

UNWORTHY.

SHAME, SHAME, YES. BUT THE HEADSMAN IS JUST.

LET US FIND OUT HOW HE JUDGES ME.

NOW WHERE... AH.

JINGLE $ $

$ $

JANGLE $

AW, COME ON!!

A BRIBE?!

THAT LOOKED AN AWFUL LOT LIKE CHEATING, SIR!

CHEATING! CHEATER, I NAME THEE !!

SIMPLY A TIP!

SHOULD WE SEND HIM HOME TO HIS FAMILY WITH EMPTY POCKETS?

I DON'T *HAVE* ANY MONEY!

THEN YOU DO NOT PASS.

THE GAME IS OV--

KA BAM

MUG!

THAT WAS WEIRD.

I FIGURED THERE'D BE A GUY IN THERE.

AH WELL. HEY KID!

I WAS GONNA COME AND RESCUE YOU!

HOW'D YOU GET OUTTA JAIL??

THE USUAL WAY. C'MON, WE GOTTA GO.

I'VE LEARNED A FEW THINGS IN JAIL.

BAD THINGS.

I THINK WE HAVE TO--

MUG, WE NEED TO QUIT THE ORDER.

I KNOW WHAT YOU'RE THINKING, BUT IT'S TRUE.

THIS IS ANOTHER CHAMPION PUNISHED WITHOUT CAUSE. THE ORDER IS ACTING UNJUSTLY. WE CAN'T BE A PART OF IT.

PLEASE, MUG, YOU HAVE TO BELIEVE ME.

OKAY.

YOU REALLY MEAN IT?

YEAH, YA KNOW, IT'S TIME FER ME TO BE MY OWN GUY.

I'M SICK A' FUSSIN' AND FIGHTIN' FER SOMEONE ELSE'S-

AHEM.

WE ARE NOT FINISHED HERE.

WHO'S THIS GUY? A GUY I GOTTA KNOCK AROUND A LITTLE?

WHAT? NO. THIS IS KING ARCHIBALD. HE LOVES GOLF, BUT ISN'T ALLOWED TO GOLF, BUT *THEN*-!

I BROKE INTO HIS CASTLE AND ACCIDENTALLY *GOLFED*.

ANYWAY, I NEED TO WIN THIS GAME OR ELSE I GET EATEN.

THAT PART'S NOT GREAT, BUT OTHERWISE, IT'S BEEN PRETTY FUN.

HMPH.

WELL, KID, THAT'S ALL VERY CONFUSING. BUT YOU NEED ANY HELP, JUST SAY THE--

ACTUALLY, COULD YOU MOVE OVER THERE FOR A SEC?

YES!

IF THAT WAS *NUMBER EIGHT*, THEN...

ALL THAT'S LEFT IS...

THE FINAL HOLE.

THERE'S NOTHING HERE.

ENTER, AND THE TRIAL WILL REVEAL ITSELF.

THIS PLACE REEKS OF BAD MAGIC.

FEH!

WILL YOU GO IN WITH ME?

WHAT, I'M GONNA SIT OUT HERE LEARNIN' FRENCH FROM THIS BIG, GREEN MONSTER?

NAH. MYSTERY DOOR IT IS.

LET'S GO.

UH.

HM.

IS THAT A...

NO WAY.

EH?

IT'S A HAT FROM MY LITTLE LEAGUE TEAM.

BUT WHAT'S IT DOING HERE?

WIZ...

MOM?

HEY! WAIT!

MOM? DAD?

WIZ...

YOU CAME BACK

TOO LATE

THE ARCH-MAGE!

NO...

NO!

NO!!

FOCUS, KID!

REMEMBER WHERE WE ARE!!

TAKE THE CLUB!!

HEY, YA DID IT, KID!!

YES, MASTERFULLY PLAYED.

I HAVE THEE TO THANK.

I THOUGHT I'D SEEN THE LAST OF MY TRUE SELF.

I WAS CERTAIN THOU WERE DONE FOR, BUT THOU DID'ST PROVE ME WRONG.

BRAVO!

...?? KING..?

AH, STILL A LITTLE FOGGY FROM THE VISIONS, I SEE.

THIS PLACE... WHAT... IS...?

WHAT IT *IS*, WELL, I'M NOT SURE.

IT WAS HERE BEFORE I ARRIVED.

WHAT IT *DOES* IS SHOW THINE OWN HEART'S MOST CRIPPLING FEAR.

SO IT'S NOT... REAL...?

NOT YET.

BUT IF YOU DO NOT FACE THAT FEAR, IT MAY COME TO PASS.

AS MINE DID.

WHAT DID YOU SEE IN THE RUINS?

I SAW MY PEOPLE HEWN BENEATH RED CLAWS.

I SAW MYSELF, A SLAVERING BEAST.

AND WHEN I LOST GOLF, MY ONE GREAT JOY, I BECAME THE BEAST I FEARED.

I BARRED THE GATES, CLUNG TO MY RECORD.

I FORGOT ALL ELSE.

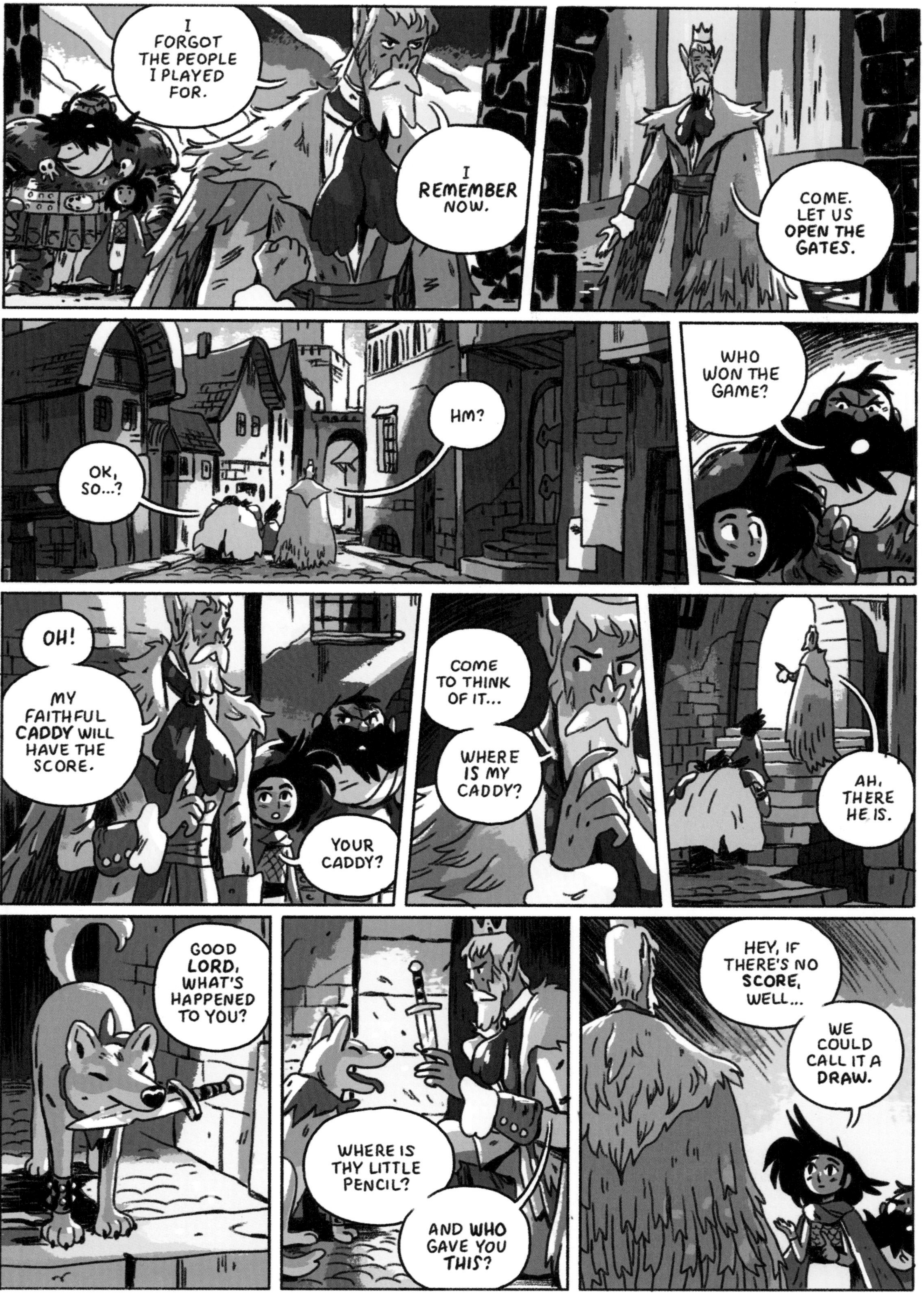
I FORGOT THE PEOPLE I PLAYED FOR.
I REMEMBER NOW.
COME. LET US OPEN THE GATES.
OK, SO...?
HM?
WHO WON THE GAME?
OH!
MY FAITHFUL CADDY WILL HAVE THE SCORE.
YOUR CADDY?
COME TO THINK OF IT...
WHERE IS MY CADDY?
AH, THERE HE IS.
GOOD LORD, WHAT'S HAPPENED TO YOU?
WHERE IS THY LITTLE PENCIL?
AND WHO GAVE YOU THIS?
HEY, IF THERE'S NO SCORE, WELL...
WE COULD CALL IT A DRAW.

A TIE?!

SO...I KEEP MY RECORD.

AND NOBODY GETS EATEN?

YEP.

YES... I THINK THAT WOULD BE FAIR.

A DRAW.

I HAVE NOT SEEN THE SUN RISE FROM OUTSIDE MY WALLS IN A VERY LONG TIME.

WHAT'LL YOU DO NOW?

FIRST I HAVE TO TELL MY MOTHER OF MY FATE.

NO DOUBT SHE THINKS I'VE BEEN EATEN.

THEN I TRY TO REGAIN MY PEOPLE'S TRUST, IF THEY WILL HAVE ME.

I WOULD NOT HAVE THIS SECOND CHANCE IF NOT FOR THEE.

PLEASE ACCEPT OUR HIGHEST HONOR.

THANK YOU!

IF IT'S NOT TOO MUCH, COULD I ASK FOR ONE MORE THING?

I THINK IT'S THIS ONE.

IF YER LOOKIN' FOR THE SEA-BEAR, YAR, THIS BE SHE.

HI! I'M WI—

KING SENT WORD. WHERE TO, THEN?

YER SURE THIS IS WHAT YA WANT, KID?

I AM.

TAKE US TO THE ARCHMAGE.

THE END

ONE LAST GAME.

F. S. IV

ISBN: 978-1-910620-18-2

ORDER FROM WWW.NOBROW.NET

ALSO IN THE SERIES...

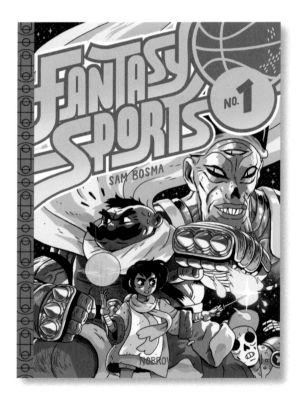

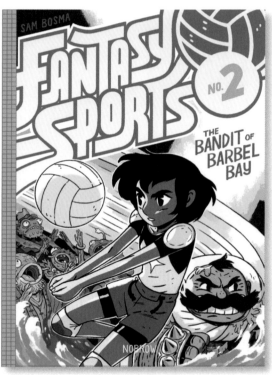

FANTASY SPORTS NO.1
ISBN: 978-1-907704-80-2

FANTASY SPORTS NO.2
ISBN: 978-1-910620-10-6

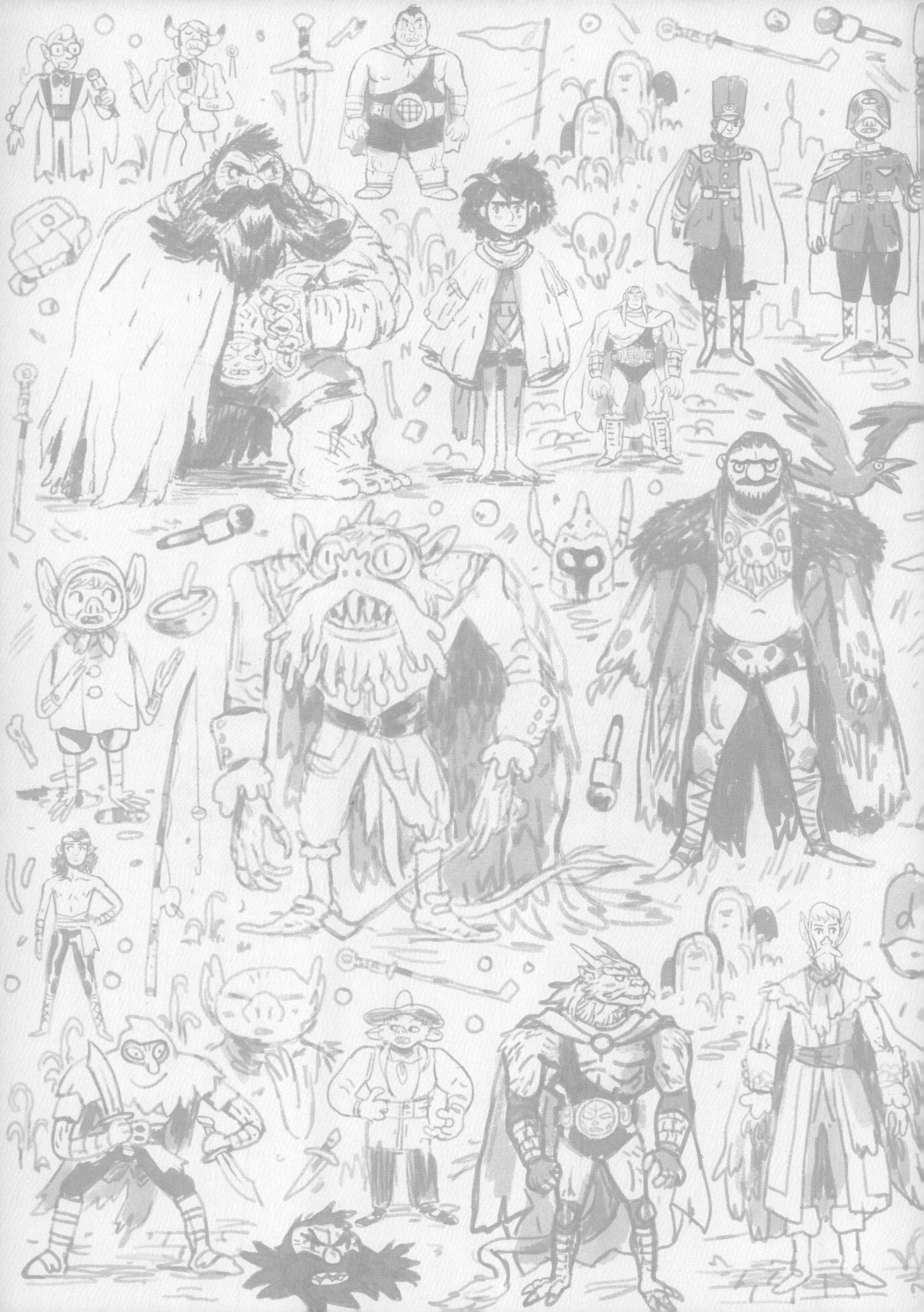